How A Spice Island Villa
Became A Village Famil

Martha Richardson

Illustrated by John Benjamin

For my family, El. Rich., Robert, Alex and Liz, with love and thanks. And for my siblings, and the precious memories we have created in our quiet village.

I also dedicate this book to my fellow Grenadian citizens. As you read the story, may you be inspired by the villagers who proved that when family, friends, and community work together in love during times of adversity, miracles happen!

-M.A.R.-

I dedicate this illustration in memory of my mother and father and equally to my two children, Donna-Maria and Helen in Holland. In addition, to all my lovely students that passed my tutelage in those rich and creative days.

-J.B-

Printed in Victoria, Canada

National Library of Canada Cataloguing in Publication Data

A cataloguing record for this book that includes the U.S. Library of Congress Classification number, the Library of Congress Call number and the Dewey Decimal cataloguing code is available from the National Library of Canada. The complete cataloguing record can be obtained from the National Library's online database at: www.nlc-bnc.ca/amicus/index-e.html

ISBN: 1-4120-3176-1

TRAFFORD

This book was published on-demand in cooperation with Trafford Publishing.
On-demand publishing is a unique process and service of making a book available for retail sale to the public taking advantage of on-demand manufacturing and Internet marketing. On-demand publishing includes promotions, retail sales, manufacturing, order fulfilment, accounting and collecting royalties on behalf of the author.

Suite 6E, 2333 Government St., Victoria, B.C. V8T 4P4, CANADA

Phone	250-383-6864	Toll-free	1-888-232-4444 (Canada & US)
Fax	250-383-6804	E-mail sales@trafford.com	
Web site	www.trafford.com	TRAFFORD PUBLISHING IS A DIVISION OF TRAFFORD HOLDINGS LTD.	
Trafford Catalogue #04-1003		www.trafford.com/robots/04-1003.html	

10   9   8   7

Once, in a quiet village on the lush, tropical spice Island, there lived a boy named Willie and his close-knit relatives.

Every Friday evening, as soon as the sun went down, Willie would bring home his goats and sheep from grazing in the pasture all day. Then he and Ma and Pa would end their day's chores. Afterwards, weather permitting, they would hold a cook-out under the starry sky to celebrate the beautiful evening with their relatives Brother Bill, Uncle Fred, Auntie Carol, and Sister Donna Lee.

Nearby, the leaves would rustle in the cool Caribbean evening breeze. Ma would stand over her coal-pot cooking a delicious feast. Uncle Fred would strum his banjo briskly; the chung-a-lung-a-lung-chung-a-lung-a-lung would blend with the deep-throated croak, croak, croak of overgrown brown frogs, and with the chirp, chirp, chirp of sprightly green crickets. Dozens of fireflies, like little dancing stars would click, click, click in the air and dazzle the sky with their flashing lights.

Holding hands in a circle under the luminous moon, the children would sway to the banjo and sing, "Suzie in the moonlight, Suzie in the dew, Suzie never come back to hear my banjo play. Walk in Suzie, walk in, walk in here I say. Walk into my parlor to hear my banjo play…."

Only then would Ma serve the family stuffed crab-backs, okroes, coo-coo, curried fried fish, and oil-down, and Pa's special brew of mauby. The mouth-watering aromas would mingle with the perfume of roses, frangipani, and jasmine, and with the lingering spicy smells of cinnamon, mace, nutmeg, and cloves, left outside earlier to dry.

After feasting on Ma's delicious food, the stuffed and drowsy adults would play a quiet game of dominoes. The children, still filled with enough energy to last another day, would pitch marbles. Sister Donna Lee would tell scary folktales, and afterwards, Uncle Fred would chase away the dreaded nightmares with lively music.

A long time passed in the quiet village. Brother Bill, Sister Donna Lee, Uncle Fred, and Auntie Carol went away with their families to live in neighboring villages. They left behind Willie, Ma and Pa, and the special Friday evening family tradition. The closeness Willie once shared with his relatives was gone. Inside him remained sadness and deep longing for his relatives, whom he saw less and less with each passing year.

Willie, Ma and Pa tried to get their relatives together again. But whenever Ma cooked a special meal and invited them to the feast, they seldom came.

When she planted new flowers in the beautiful garden and sent Willie to ask them to come and admire them, they hardly came.

And every year at the village fair, Willie, Ma and Pa
would search the crowds for their relatives, but it was in vain.

One day Willie sat on the bank of a river quietly tossing
sticks into its clear, rippling water. Every now and then he
would wade into the water and snatch the sticks before they
drifted away forever. As if a light had suddenly switched on
in his head, Willie realized that just as he had saved the sticks
from drifting down the river, he could save his family from
drifting apart any further. He jumped out of the water and
raced home as fast as his legs could carry him.

"Is not too late Ma. Is not too late Pa," Willie announced to his parents. "I could still bring we family together."

Pouring him a glass of cool, coconut water, Ma said, "In that case, hurry up nuh boy. Go and talk to them 'fore it get dark."

Traveling to the villages to see his relatives, Willie sometimes ran on flat road; at times he climbed steep hills. Sometimes he took short-cuts through narrow, tree-lined, stony paths and dusty trails. Thinking about the reunion he would have with his relatives, his heart sang for joy. He was oblivious to the loud barking of dogs and the soreness in his feet from walking and running on loose stones.

Every now and then he would stop at the top of a hill to admire the lush, green vegetation and the flat, red-roofed, brightly painted houses below.

In the distance he could see the small town, fishing boats, and regal sailboats gliding on the calm, turquoise water.

"Good afternoon. Good afternoon," Willie politely greeted villagers, young and old, along the way.

As he passed house after house, he could smell mouth-watering aromas of split pea soup, curried goat, and other delicious smells wafting from kitchens; he could see food cooking on coal pots out in the yards.

At last, Willie came to Uncle Fred's house. Not surprisingly, Uncle Fred was polishing his instruments.

"Sorry Willie boy. I going to have to miss dis fair. Me and de boys have to practice for a big show next week," Uncle Fred explained.

Disappointed, and fighting back tears, Willie headed to see Auntie Carol.

But when he arrived, Auntie Carol was loading her truck to go on a trip.

"Is no way I could go to de fair, Willie. I done plan my day already. I just can't go dis time," Auntie Carol explained.

Even Brother Bill had an excuse.

 "I have to conserve all my energy to play my next big cricket match," he told Willie.

Sad, but determined, Willie trudged on to see Sister Donna Lee.

"De village fair!" shrieked Sister Donna Lee. "But I still working on my important story. I can't go to de fair!"

Poor Willie was disappointed. He and Ma and Pa had tried their best to reunite the family. But it was no use. After all this time the family still had not gotten together.

"Uncle Fred have his music, Auntie Carol have her trips, Brother Bill have his cricket match, and Sister Donna Lee have her stories," Willie thought as he headed home. "Everyone too busy to visit; they even too busy to come to the village fair. Nothing will ever bring we family together again."

Early the next morning Willie was awakened by howling winds banging windows and doors, snapping off branches, and uprooting trees in the quiet village. He could hear rain drumming on the galvanized rooftop, swooshing down the spouting, and overflowing ditches.

Later that day the skies cleared, and once more the sun smiled upon the quiet village. It slowly soaked up the soggy ground. But the quiet village was a collage of broken branches and litter. The site chosen for the fair looked more like a dumpsite.

"We need everybody help to clean up dis mess in time for de fair!" declared Willie.

Suddenly he thought about his relatives. He thought about the things they enjoyed doing; things that took up plenty of their time—things that other villagers would also enjoy doing—at the fair.

The next afternoon, Ma drove Willie to the villages to
see their relatives once more.

When Willie told Uncle Fred, Auntie Carol, Brother Bill, and Sister Donna Lee his idea, they were very excited; immediately they returned with him and Ma to help clean up after the storm.

The next day the quiet village bustled with villagers and visitors. All day long, Willie's relatives worked together to entertain everyone at the fair. They could not remember the last time they had worked together like this. They were overjoyed by the love and admiration they still felt for one another.

Other village families couldn't help but be impressed.

As for His Excellency Governor General and his dignitaries, they were impressed by this fair as they've been impressed by no other.

The lively steel band music, the variety of foods cooked so deliciously, the imaginative stories told to the children, the energizing games, and the huge tent which shaded people from the scorching sun— overwhelmed the governor!

He called his dignitaries together for a brief meeting. If there was one thing the governor always did, it was to reward others for a job well done.

"Today, this quiet village has set a precedent in village fairs," began the governor. "Instead of the usual fair, you have worked together to make this fair extraordinary. So I am happy to reward this here, young boy, Willie, for organizing the village cleanup in time for the fair. I also commend each of you for showing love and commitment to this quiet village, and most important, to family. You are true neighbors!"

The governor paused, and someone shouted,

"Is no way we could call we self neighbors or family, for dat matter, if we don't show one ounce ah love for one anodder."

The people cheered, and the governor continued his speech.

"From now on, instead of an ordinary fair, this village shall celebrate a Village Family Affair. All village families shall have this special day to celebrate each other, to entertain, and be entertained together."

The villagers felt proud for informing the governor that Willie was responsible for getting his family to help clean up the village in time for the fair. They commended one another for letting His Excellency know that Ma's food had kept up everyone's energy to play Brother Bill's games; that Uncle Fred's music had given rhythm to Sister Donna Lee's stories which fascinated the children; that it was Auntie Carol's huge tent that shaded and united families from other villages.

A few months later, the first-ever Spice Island Village Family Affair Committee was formed, and Willie was personally invited by His Excellency Governor General himself to serve on the committee along with his relatives and other villagers.

From that day on, Willie lived an extraordinary life.

About The "Spice Island"

Grenada, a tiny Caribbean island became known as the Spice Island for its abundance of spices which include cinnamon, allspice, cloves, ginger, vanilla bean and bay leaf. Nutmeg, which first began to thrive in the island in the mid-nineteenth century continued to prosper in Grenada, making it the world's second largest producer. The islanders usually grow their own spices for seasoning food, flavoring drinks, and for baking cakes. They also boil dried cinnamon sticks to make a spicy and delicious hot "tea."

At only 133 square miles (twice the size of Washington, D.C.), this volcanic Caribbean island situated between the Caribbean Sea and the Atlantic Ocean, is one of the smallest in the Western Hemisphere. It includes the tiny outlying islands of Carriacou and Petite Martinique.

Grenada boasts a tropical climate with an average temperature of 75 degrees Fahrenheit, tempered by North East Trade Winds. The island has only two seasons: the wet season which lasts from June to December, and the dry season which lasts from January to May.

The leaders of the island include the Head of State Queen Elizabeth II, represented by a governor general, and the prime minister. In 1983 the island's leader was overthrown and executed, causing US forces to invade the island on a rescue mission. The US, together with other Caribbean Islands, successfully restored peace to Grenada.

Glossary of words in the story

Coal pot—a round, open-top cast iron pot used for cooking indoors or outdoors. Coal is placed on a middle grate and lit with fuel. After the fire gets going, a pot for cooking is placed on top of the coal

Cook-out—a barbecue with Caribbean dishes

Coo-coo—a dish made from ground corn, okroes and coconut milk, similar to polenta

Cricket—a popular game played in the Caribbean and Europe, similar to baseball, but played with wickets and eleven players on each team

Curried goat—goat meat stewed and seasoned with curry and other island spices

Mace—the red, lace-like outer covering of the nutmeg nut

Mauby—a drink made by boiling mauby bark in water, flavored with sugar and aniseed, and served cold

Oil-down—the national dish of Grenada, this one-pot meal is a combination of salt meat, local vegetables, seasonings and dumplings stewed in coconut milk

Okroes (okras)—a long, pointed end, narrow, ridged vegetable used either as a side dish, cooked in meat, or combined with corn meal to make coo-coo

Salt fish—cod fish stewed with onions, garlic, tomatoes, cucumbers and peppers

Make Stuffed Crab-Backs!

8 crab shells or ramekins
8 ounces fresh crabmeat
½ medium onion chopped or
I tablespoon dried chopped onions
I teaspoon garlic powder or minced garlic
I tablespoon fresh or dried thyme
I tablespoon fresh chopped scallion or chive
3 slices bread soaked or ½ cup bread crumbs
¼ teaspoon black pepper
1 tablespoon curry powder

1. Wash and scrub crab backs with water and vinegar. Boil 15 minutes in water with 1 tablespoon salt. Grease shells with butter or oil.
2. Preheat oven at 350˚ for 15 minutes. Flake crab meat and mix in all ingredients, adding salt to taste.
3. Spoon mixture into crab backs and garnish with curry powder. Top with crumbled soaked bread and bake for 10 minutes. Serves 8.

Pitch Marbles!

(2 to 5 players)

1. Select a dry, smooth surface (outdoor or indoor) and draw a circle using spray paint or chalk, or by tracing a line with a stick, or by using string.
2. Measure 18-20 feet away from the circle and draw a horizontal line.
3. Each player places 1-5 marbles in the circle and keeps one shooter (large marble) or alley (small marble) for shooting.
4. Players stand on the horizontal line and take turns rolling one marble to knock out marbles in the circle. As long as a player keeps knocking out marbles, his turn continues. However, he loses his turn if he misses. Player keeps the marbles he knocks out.
5. Player shoots his marble from any location where it has landed. He may choose to knock out marbles from the circle or try to shoot another player's marble outside the circle. If he knocks a player's marble, he takes one from the circle. The player with the most marbles wins the game. More players may be added at the end of the round or a new game may be started by repeating the procedure.

About The Author

Growing up in a Grenadian countryside, Martha Richardson played games, sang folk songs, and listened to folk tales with her parents, 13 siblings, cousins, and village friends under the starry sky.

After graduating from high school, Martha taught elementary school for two years, and then migrated to the U.S. A. where she studied journalism and business administration. During her college years, the author spent as much time studying children's literature as she did journalism.

Over the years, the author has worked in many capacities including: newspaper reporter, teacher, library assistant and TV producer/reporter. This is her first children's book.

She lives in New Jersey with her husband and three children.

About The Illustrator

John Benjamin taught Martha Richardson art in Grenada from first grade through high school during his service as visiting art tutor for elementary and secondary schools, and also as supervisor of art in the Ministry of Education. When Martha became an elementary school teacher, John Benjamin taught her students art. Now this former art tutor and his student have reunited as illustrator and author.

One of the Caribbean's renowned master painters, Benjamin has received numerous awards for his work which has been exhibited throughout the Caribbean and abroad, including: England, France, Germany, Italy, The Americas, Canada, Japan, and Switzerland.

In 1997, a collection stamp of his work was printed and commemorated in his honor by Lausanne, Switzerland. He has also received a medal of honor from Tokyo for "outstanding illustration of a children's picture book."

The artist is a member of the Most Excellent Order of the British Empire (M.B.E.).

He lives in Grenada.